Stuck in
the mud

written by Shirley Jackson
illustrated by Jan Smith

In the machine,

out of the machine.

On the line,

off the line.

In the mud,

out of the mud.

Back in the machine!

Soggy socks

written by Lorraine Horsley
illustrated by Julie Anderson

I put on my socks and

I put on my T-shirt.

I put on my jeans and

I put on my jumper.

I put on my gloves and

I put on my hat.

Whoops, no boots!

Messy mud!

written by Catriona Macgregor
illustrated by David Melling

Ben was in
the mud.

Ben was in
the kitchen.

Ben was in
the sitting room.

Ben was in
the hall.

Ben was in
the bathroom.

Ben was in
the bedroom.

Ben was
in trouble.

Rollercoaster ride

written by Shirley Jackson
illustrated by Tania Hurt-Newton

Up, up, up,
slow, slow, slow,

down, down, down, away we go!

Round and round,

fast, fast, fast,

down, down, down,

back at last!

New words introduced in this book

bathroom   bedroom   hall

kitchen

sitting room

gloves   jeans   jumper

at, away, back, Ben, down,
out, put, round, trouble,